GOSCINNY AND UDERZO

PRESENT

Fourteen all-new Asterix stories

Asterix
and the class act

Written by RENÉ GOSCINNY
and ALBERT UDERZO

Illustrated by ALBERT UDERZO

Translated by ANTHEA BELL *and* DEREK HOCKRIDGE

The French publisher's note

During the 1960s, when René Goscinny and Albert Uderzo had time to spare from writing and drawing the longer Asterix adventures ... which was not very often ... they produced some little masterpieces in the form of complete short stories. The French magazine "Pilote", enjoyed by a whole generation of children, in which the Asterix stories first appeared, published most but not all of them. Others appeared in such places as American newspapers, a women's magazine, and as part of a bid for the Olympic Games to be held in Paris. It seemed a good idea to collect all these short stories in a special Asterix album — in fact here at Les Éditions Albert René, we were receiving such terrible threats that we absolutely had to do it. If we didn't publish them, said readers, they would make us eat roast boar for breakfast! So we gave in to the outrageous demands of certain blackmailers whose identity we shall have to reveal one of these days.

But for the moment, having brought these lost treasures to light, we hope you will enjoy reading them. Some of the stories in this book are both written and illustrated by Albert on his own, because they were created after the death in 1977 of his friend and colleague, the other half of the most famous strip cartoon team in the world: René Goscinny and Albert Uderzo.

None of these stories had been published in English before, although several were included in our 1993 collection (see page 47 for the full story).

Seeing his publishers absorbed in the difficult but fascinating task of collecting the stories and improving the original picture quality for "Asterix and the Class Act", Albert set to work again. And in the spring of 2003 he produced the cover design and the words and drawings for a brand-new five-page story, about a cockerel with amazing powers. Will the rooster who wakes the Gauls every morning rouse the children of today to get up and go to school for their own class act?

Original title: *Astérix et la rentrée gauloise*
Original edition © 2003 Les Éditions Albert René / Goscinny-Uderzo
English translation © 2003 Les Éditions Albert René / Goscinny-Uderzo

Exclusive licensee: Orion Publishing Group • Translators: Anthea Bell and Derek Hockridge • Typography: Bryony Newhouse • Co-ordination: Studio 'Et Cetera'

All rights reserved

This edition first published in Great Britain in 2003 by Orion Books Ltd, Orion House, 5 Upper St Martin's Lane, London WC2H 9EA
An Hachette UK company

3 5 7 9 10 8 6 4

Printed in China

www.asterix.com   www.orionbooks.co.uk

A CIP Catalogue record for this book is available from the British Library

ISBN 978-0-7528-6068-8 (cased) • ISBN 978-0-7528-6640-6 (paperback) • ISBN 978-1-4440-1339-9 (ebook)

The Orion Publishing Group's policy is to use papers that are natural, renewable and recyclable products and made from wood grown in sustainable forests. The logging and manufacturing processes are expected to conform to the environmental regulations of the country of origin.

GAULISH VILLAGE

COMPENDIUM

LAUDANUM

AQUARIUM

TOTORUM

ARMORICA

BELGICA

LUTETIA

GAUL
(ROMAN CONQUEST)
50 BC

CELTICA

AQUITANIA

PROVINCIA

THE YEAR IS 50 BC. GAUL IS ENTIRELY OCCUPIED BY THE
ROMANS. WELL, NOT ENTIRELY ... ONE SMALL VILLAGE OF
INDOMITABLE GAULS STILL HOLDS OUT AGAINST THE INVADERS.
AND LIFE IS NOT EASY FOR THE ROMAN LEGIONARIES WHO
GARRISON THE FORTIFIED CAMPS OF TOTORUM, AQUARIUM,
LAUDANUM AND COMPENDIUM ...

ASTERIX, THE HERO OF THESE ADVENTURES. A SHREWD, CUNNING LITTLE WARRIOR, ALL PERILOUS MISSIONS ARE IMMEDIATELY ENTRUSTED TO HIM. ASTERIX GETS HIS SUPERHUMAN STRENGTH FROM THE MAGIC POTION BREWED BY THE DRUID GETAFIX . . .

OBELIX, ASTERIX'S INSEPARABLE FRIEND. A MENHIR DELIVERY MAN BY TRADE, ADDICTED TO WILD BOAR. OBELIX IS ALWAYS READY TO DROP EVERYTHING AND GO OFF ON A NEW ADVENTURE WITH ASTERIX – SO LONG AS THERE'S WILD BOAR TO EAT, AND PLENTY OF FIGHTING. HIS CONSTANT COMPANION IS DOGMATIX, THE ONLY KNOWN CANINE ECOLOGIST, WHO HOWLS WITH DESPAIR WHEN A TREE IS CUT DOWN.

GETAFIX, THE VENERABLE VILLAGE DRUID, GATHERS MISTLETOE AND BREWS MAGIC POTIONS. HIS SPECIALITY IS THE POTION WHICH GIVES THE DRINKER SUPERHUMAN STRENGTH. BUT GETAFIX ALSO HAS OTHER RECIPES UP HIS SLEEVE . . .

CACOFONIX, THE BARD. OPINION IS DIVIDED AS TO HIS MUSICAL GIFTS. CACOFONIX THINKS HE'S A GENIUS. EVERY-ONE ELSE THINKS HE'S UNSPEAKABLE. BUT SO LONG AS HE DOESN'T SPEAK, LET ALONE SING, EVERYBODY LIKES HIM . . .

FINALLY, VITALSTATISTIX, THE CHIEF OF THE TRIBE. MAJESTIC, BRAVE AND HOT-TEMPERED, THE OLD WARRIOR IS RESPECTED BY HIS MEN AND FEARED BY HIS ENEMIES. VITALSTATISTIX HIMSELF HAS ONLY ONE FEAR, HE IS AFRAID THE SKY MAY FALL ON HIS HEAD TOMORROW. BUT AS HE ALWAYS SAYS, TOMORROW NEVER COMES.

DEAR READERS, I AM DELIGHTED TO SEE SO MANY OF YOU HERE ... I KNOW SOME OF YOU WANT TO PUT A FEW QUESTIONS TO ME, CHIEF VITALSTATISTIX, SO FIRE AWAY!

YES?

WILL YOUR NEXT ADVENTURE BE ABROAD OR AT HOME?

WILL YOU PLAY AN IMPORTANT PART IN IT YOURSELF?

THANK YOU ...

WILL IT BE AS FUNNY AND EXCITING AS THE OTHER STORIES? WILL THE ROMANS GET A GOOD THUMPING?

IS THAT ALL?

RIGHT ... YOU WANT TO KNOW WHERE THE STORY WILL TAKE PLACE, IF I SHALL PLAY A LEADING PART, AND IF THE ROMANS WILL GET A GOOD THUMPING ...

THIS IS A COLLECTION OF SEVERAL STORIES TAKING PLACE IN AND AROUND OUR BELOVED VILLAGE ... AS YOUR LEADER *OF COURSE* I SHALL PLAY A STATISTICALLY VITAL PART AND, YES, THE ROMANS WILL CERTAINLY GET A GOOD THUMPING!

DID I HEAR SOMEONE ASK WHEN OUR ADVENTURES WILL BEGIN?

AS SOON AS YOU TAKE THE TROUBLE TO TURN THIS PAGE! THANK YOU FOR YOUR KIND ATTENTION!

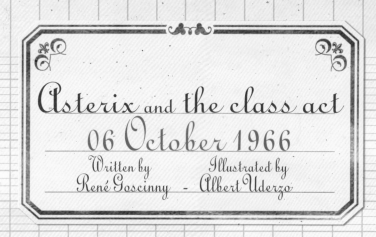

Asterix and the class act
06 October 1966

Written by
René Goscinny - Illustrated by **Albert Uderzo**

The magazine "Pilote" published 52 issues a year, so the editorial team had to rack its brains to think up new stories every week.

When the beginning of the new school year came round, it seemed an ideal subject. René and Albert thought about the logistical problems facing the Gauls in getting their children to school. Here we see them, rather in advance of their time, using the equivalent of the school bus in the year 50 BC. René sat down at his typewriter and soon sent Albert the text. "One of René's talents," Albert Uderzo still remembers, "was a gift for adaptin his stories for different artists. Morris hated wordplay, so René didn't use it in the "Luc Luke" cowboy stories that Morris illustrated. Tabary, who illustrated René's stories abo the wicked Arabian Nights vizier "Iznogo loved puns, so those books are full of them There was total sympathy and understand between René and Albert, who were gre friends and equal partners. They never f the slightest anxiety about the quality each other's work. The cover of the magazine "Pilote" was created by Albert.

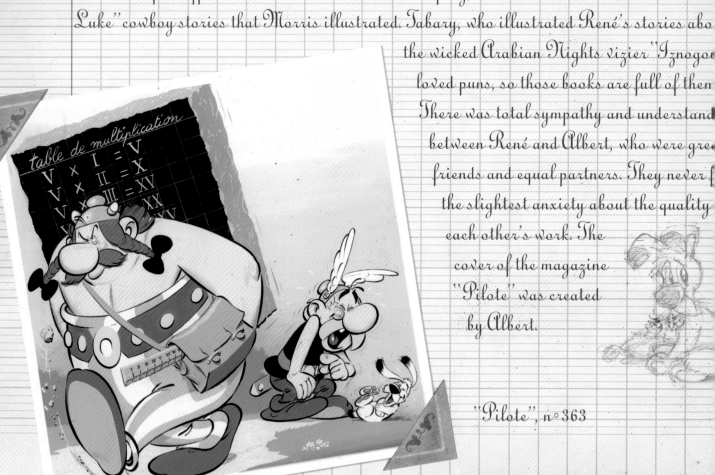

"Pilote", n° 363

The birth of Asterix
October 1994

Written and illustrated by Albert Uderzo

To celebrate 35 years of Asterix stories, we decided to publish an Asterix Special for the little Gaul's birthday, a one-off magazine in the spirit of "Pilote" in the 1960s. We got together famous names and European authors who wanted to pay tribute to Asterix and his friends. As part of our project, of course, we hoped for a new Asterix story.

It was in a plane bound for Copenhagen in the spring of 1994 that Albert Uderzo told us, with relish, about his idea for an original story to celebrate the birthday. He was already looking forward to revealing the secret of the birth of Asterix and Obelix, and at the same time he told us the names of the older generation: Asterix's parents Astronomix and Sarsaparilla, and Obelix's father and mother Obeliscoidix and Vanilla.

"Le Journal exceptionnel d'Astérix"

IN THE YEAR 35 B.C.*

* BEFORE CAESAR

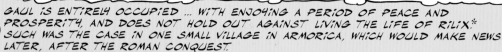

GAUL IS ENTIRELY OCCUPIED ... WITH ENJOYING A PERIOD OF PEACE AND PROSPERITY, AND DOES NOT HOLD OUT AGAINST LIVING THE LIFE OF RILIX.* SUCH WAS THE CASE IN ONE SMALL VILLAGE IN ARMORICA, WHICH WOULD MAKE NEWS LATER, AFTER THE ROMAN CONQUEST.

* ANCIENT GAUL KNOWN FOR HIS LOVE OF LUXURY

COMING OUT TO PLAY, VITALSTATISTIX?

ALL RIGHT, BUT REMEMBER I'M THE CHIEF!

SO WHY ITH IT ALWAYTH YOU WHO PLAYTH THE CHIEF?

BECAUSE MY DAD IS THE CHIEF OF THIS VILLAGE. HE'S THE BOSS! THAT'S WHY!

OH YEAH? WELL, MY DAD SAYTH YOUR DAD OUGHT TO BE MATHTER IN HITH OWN HOUTHE BEFORE BOTHING THE VILLAGE ABOUT!

WHAT WAS THAT?

SAY THAT AGAIN IF YOU DARE!

I'M ABOUT TO LOTHE MY TEMPER, THO WATCH OUT!

HE'S RIGHT!

NO, HE'S WRONG!

HE'S RIGHT!

NO, HE'S WRONG!

CLUCK! SQUAWK!

BANG! BANG!

PUT THAT CHICKEN DOWN, YOU FOUL PESTS!

AREN'T YOU ASHAMED OF YOURSELVES, FIGHTING LIKE LITTLE BARBARIANS?

SQUAWK!

AND HERE WE SEE THE VERY FIRST IN A LONG SERIES OF FISH FIGHTS IN THE GAULISH VILLAGE.

YOU SHOULD BE ASHAMED OF YOUR-SELVES, FIGHTING IN FRONT OF YOUR CHILDREN!

MEANWHILE ...

OFF YOU GO, ASTRONOMIX! THIS IS NO PLACE FOR YOU! LEAVE IT ALL TO US!

DO BE SENSIBLE, OBELISCOIDIX, YOU WON'T BE ANY USE IN THERE

IT'S GALLING FOR A GAUL TO BE SO HELPLESS AT A TIME LIKE THIS, DON'T YOU THINK, OBELISCOIDIX?

YUP ... AND WHEN I FEEL GALLED I GET HUNGRY!

SPLATCH!

FOLLOW ME! THIS WILL CALM US DOWN!

STOP THAT! THIS IS NO DAY FOR VULGAR BRAWLS!

12

In 50 BC
May 1977

Written by
René Goscinny

Illustrated by
Albert Uderzo

Georges Dargaud, the publisher of "Pilote" and the Asterix books, wanted to see his leading series reach the American market. The head of an American syndicate visited Paris to meet the creators of the phenomenally successful character Asterix, and they soon came an agreement. An Asterix album would be published in daily instalments in a number of American papers. René and Albert were delighted but cautious, and thought it might be a good idea to present the world of Asterix to the Americans in an original, condensed form before embarking on the publication of a whole story. The result was these three pages, whi for a long time were unknown even in France. Enjoy!

It was the famous "National Geographic" magazine that published them in May 197 when it was running a major piece about the Gauls. However, the authors' efforts went unrewarded. Publication in American strip cartoon format meant reducing the size of the pictures, which made it difficult to read the speech bubbles. As the authors did not want to have their original work modified beyond the adaptations usual in translation, the experiment ended after the first album — since René and Albert declined an offer for them go and live in the USA so as to suit their work to the "American format".

ONE SUCH GROUP OF GAULS WAS HOLDING OUT IN A TINY VILLAGE ON THE WEST COAST OF THE COUNTRY.

THE ROMANS KEPT A CLOSE WATCH ON THESE CHEERFUL GAULS, WHO LIKED A GOOD LAUGH ...

BY JUPITER, THE GAULS SEEM TO GO IN FOR KNOCKABOUT FARCE!

OF ALL THE VILLAGE WARRIORS, ASTERIX WAS THE MOST INTELLIGENT ...

... AND THE BEST AT UNMASKING ROMAN SPIES.

BY JUPITER, HOW DID HE SEE THROUGH MY CUNNING DISGUISE?

I TOLD YOU OAK TREES DO SMELL OF GAR GEORGE!

OBELIX, A MENHIR DELIVERY MAN BY TRADE, IS ASTERIX'S BEST FRIEND.

HISTORIANS HAVE NOT YET FOUND OUT WHAT MENHIRS WERE ACTUALLY FOR.

AND AS FOR THE USE OBELIX OFTEN MAKES OF THEM, THE ROMANS AS WELL AS HISTORIANS ARE AT CROSS PURPOS

CROSS, BY JUPITER? I'M FURIOUS! THIS IS NOT WHAT I'D CALL LIGHT BANTER!

LOOK, ASTERIX! I'VE TAUGHT DOGMATIX A NEW TRICK!

THIS MAY SEEM STRANGE, BUT REMEMBER THAT DOG BISCUITS HAD NOT YET BEEN INVENTED IN 50 BC.

SMACK!!?

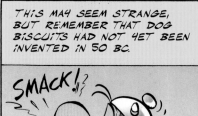

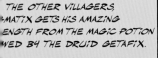

THE OTHER VILLAGERS, ...MATIX GETS HIS AMAZING ...RENGTH FROM THE MAGIC POTION ...WED BY THE DRUID GETAFIX.

THIS MAGIC POTION HAS A SPECTACULAR EFFECT ON THE GAULS ...

YOU KNOW DOGMATIX HATES PEOPLE TO PULL UP TREES!

BUT I ONLY GAVE IT A TINY TAP!

... AND THE ROMANS TOO.

BY JUPITER, THAT GAULISH BREW PACKS A PUNCH!

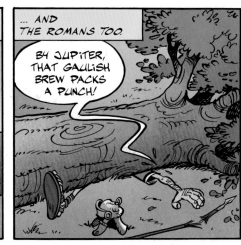

...E BARD CACOFONIX IS ...OTHER PROMINENT VILLAGER ...

OH TO BE IN ARMORICA NOW THAT APRIL'S ...

.... HERE!

... AND SO IS FULLIAUTOMATIX THE BLACKSMITH, WHO IS ALSO PROBABLY THE ANCESTOR OF ALL MUSIC CRITICS.

...E VILLAGE CHIEF IS THE ...JESTIC VITALSTATISTIX ...

THERE'S NO DISCIPLINE IN THIS VILLAGE ANY MORE! NO RESPECT! YOU ARE ALL TO BOW TO ME AND MY AUTHORITY!

BUT CHIEF, YOU SAID YOURSELF ...

I WANTED THE OTHERS TO BOW, YOU FOOLS, NOT YOU!

...THERE IS NOTHING THE ROMANS ...N DO ABOUT THE SUPERHUMAN ...RENGTH OF THE GAULISH VILLAGERS ...

...BY JUPITER, TO THINK ...ERE'S XVIII YEARS TO GO ...EFORE I'M DEMOBBED!

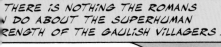

THE GAULS (OR MOST OF THEM) REMAIN FREE AND HAPPY.

UDERZO & GOSCINNY

17

Chanticleerix
August 2003

Written and illustrated by Albert Uderzo

Never before published, this five-page story was finished in May 2003 and is about the village cockerel. It adds to Albert Uderzo's carnival of animals. He has always been particularly fond of chickens. Every Asterix album contains hens and cockerels leading their private and obviously harmonious family lives in the corners of the pictures. The idea for this story came from a projected film spin-off. With René Goscinny, Albert Uderzo once planned a pilot for an animated cartoon film starring Dogmatix — a rarity which has remained unknown. But when he looked at it again 30 years later, Albert thought he would like to write a new story about the birds who share the village with the indomitable Gauls. You might think that the magical forest of Broceliande, not far from the Gaulish village, had given them new powers — but don't tell Obelix!

Gaulis
Cocker

HANTICLEERIX
THE Gaulish Cockerel
— UDERZO —

It is often thought that animals have their own language and understand each other. We see the proof of it in the following story, which begins in the skies of Armorica, just above a little village that we know well.

Teehee! Those Gauls have provided my imperial majesty with a fine appetizer!

CHILDREN! QUICK! GET UNDER COVER!

CLUCK!

?!

What is it, Mummy?

It's a nasty bird who carries off baby chicks to eat them, that's what it is!

Ha! A black chick still in the open! He's going cheap!

CHEEP! CHEEP!!

None of that! Shut your big beak or you'll feel mine in short pecking order!!!

CRAAASH

SKIDDDD

Ho, ho, ho! You think a foul fowl like you scares me? Why, you can't even fly!

Maybe not, but I am the emblem of the Gauls, I'll have you know, mister!

Then let me tell you, Galli-narius Minus, that I am the emblem of the Roman Empire!

You know what Gallithingummy Minus says to you?

GO BOIL AN EGG AND YOUR IMPERIAL HEAD TOO!

THE END

23

For Gaul Lang Syne
07 December 1967

Written by · Illustrated by
René Goscinny — Albert Uderzo

The issue of "Pilote" published at the end of the year always had to be about New Year customs...

This time René thought it would be a good idea if the Gauls joined in. He suggested to Albert reinventing an old custom dating back to Druid traditions: kissing under the mistletoe. In "Asterix the Legionary" Obelix fell in love with the beautiful Panacea, so the authors enjoyed going back to the subject. This time Obelix actually dares to try snatching a kiss, a very unusual situation for him ... but a skilful move thwarts his intentions. In condensed form, this story expresses all René Goscinny's delicacy of feeling and sense of humour, and the tender, beautiful line of Albert Uderzo's drawing.

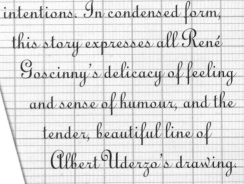

"Pilote", n° 424

or Gaul Lang Syne

THE ANCIENT GAULS HAD SOME CHARMING NEW YEAR CUSTOMS ...

WHEN TWO GAULS MET UNDER THE MISTLETOE THEY KISSED EACH OTHER.

KISSY KISSY

SMACK!

IN FACT IT WAS COMPULSORY FOR GAULS TO KISS WHEN THEY MET.

BUT I WAS SINGING, SO I ...

SINGING? YOU COULD HAVE FOOLED ME! WELL, THAT WAS YOUR KISMET!

ESE PLEASING COUNTERS WERE EER COINCIDENCE ...

GO AND PLAY, DOGMATIX! GO ON, PLAY WITH ASTERIX! I BUSY! THIS IS NOT FOR THE EYES OF LITTLE DOGS!

BUT SOME UNSCRUPULOUS GAULS LENT COINCIDENCE A HELPING HAND.

GOOD, HERE COMES PANACEA! OFF WE GO!

WHERE ARE YOU GOING, PANACEA?

I'M JUST TAKING OUR DRUID GETAFIX SOME DRY FIREWOOD.

GOING THAT AY! I'LL TAKE T FOR YOU.

OH, THANKS, SCARLATINA!

KISSY KISSY

SMACK!

OOH, I SAY, OBELIX!

?!

CAESAR'S GIVEN ORDERS. WE'RE TO RESPECT THE LOCAL CUSTOMS OF OCCUPIED COUNTRIES. SO I'M RESPECTING THEM!

Mini Midi Maxi
02 August 1971

Written by   Illustrated by
René Goscinny - Albert Uderzo

In view of the huge success of Asterix and his friends, the weekly magazine "Elle" asked the authors to provide a story on a women's subject for one of their summer issues.

Although it is true that the village of indomitable Gauls is rather a male society, the authors progressively introduced heroines into the story as regular characters, for instance Impedimenta the chief's wife, Mrs Geriatrix (the star of this two-page story), Panacea and Cleopatra.

So it would be wrong to call the authors of the Asterix books anti-feminist! In fact women play a much more important part than in many other famous series! And if the humour sometimes gently mocks them, it certainly doesn't spare the men either. Look at the rather unflattering pictures of Chief Vitalstatistix, Unhygienix the fishmonger or Fulliautomatix the village blacksmith! Thank you!

"Elle" n° 1337

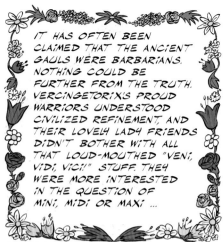

IT HAS OFTEN BEEN CLAIMED THAT THE ANCIENT GAULS WERE BARBARIANS. NOTHING COULD BE FURTHER FROM THE TRUTH. VERCINGETORIX'S PROUD WARRIORS UNDERSTOOD CIVILIZED REFINEMENT, AND THEIR LOVELY LADY FRIENDS DIDN'T BOTHER WITH ALL THAT LOUD-MOUTHED "VENI, VIDI, VICI!" STUFF. THEY WERE MORE INTERESTED IN THE QUESTION OF MINI, MIDI OR MAXI ...

FOR INSTANCE, TAKE THIS CHARMING GAULISH LADY ...

OR NO ... LET'S TAKE THIS ONE!

NOTICE THE NATURAL ELEGANCE OF HER FIGURE ...

... AND THE INFINITE CARE SHE HAS TAKEN WITH HER HAIRSTYLE.

I'M A CELEBRITY! GET ME BACK IN THERE!

AND NOW TO STUDY GAULISH FASHIONS ...

I MEAN, I AM THE CHIEF'S WIFE!

GAULISH WOMEN WORE A TUNIC ...

LOOK, IMPEDIMENTA, WOULD YOU MIND LEAVING US ALONE? CAN'T YOU SEE WE'RE BUSY?

WHAT WAS THAT?

SOMETIMES WITH A SECOND TUNIC WORN OVER IT ...

YOU LITTLE MADAM! WHO SAYS YOU CAN TALK TO ME LIKE THAT?

GERIATRIX, SWEETIE!

... IN AN ELEGANTLY MATCHING COLOUR.

WHAT'S THE MATTER, POPSY?

POPSY HERE IS A PROPER LITTLE MADAM, THAT'S WHAT

THE CLOSE-FITTING ATTRACTIVELY LOW-CUT BODICE ...

GERIATRIX, HONEYBUN, ARE YOU GOING TO LET HER SAY THOSE THINGS?

WELL ... ER ... NO ... LISTEN, IMPEDIMENTA ...

VITALSTATISTIX!

... WAS CAUGHT IN AT THE WAIST BY A BELT WITH AN ELABORATELY DESIGNED BUCKLE.

DID YOU CALL ME, IMPEDIMENTA DEAR?

THAT OLD WRECK INSULTED ME!

WHO ARE YOU CALLING AN OLD WRECK?!

E GAULISH WOMAN OFTEN WEARS DRAPERY IN THE ROMAN [...]LE, THUS ADDING AN ARISTOCRATIC TOUCH TO HER OUTFIT.

WHAT?!

WHAT'S ALL THIS SHOUTING ABOUT?

THIS LITTLE MADAM TOOK MY PLACE ...

ET DOWN F THERE YOU'RE A MAN!

LET US ALSO ADMIRE HER JEWELLERY ...

TELL ME HONESTLY, BACTERIA, DO YOU THINK SHE'S PRETTIER THAN ME?

YES.

HAS-BEEN! FOSSIL! DILAPIDATED OLD CODGER!

WANT TO FEEL THE WRONG END OF MY STICK?

ICH IS ALWAYS IN QUISITE TASTE.

NHYGIENIX!

?!

IT IS MADE OF METAL, BONE OR GLASS ...

CALM DOWN, CALM DOWN!

WHAT BUSINESS IS IT OF YOURS, YOU GREAT GOOF?

EGANT GAULISH LADIES LOVE CKLACES, BRACELETS AND BROOCHES ...

VEN THE CHIEF AS NO RIGHT TO ALL ME A GREAT GOOF!

PLATCH!

... WHICH ARE MASTERPIECES OF BEAUTY AND DISTINCTION.

COME ON, QUICK, OBELIX! THERE'S A PUNCH-UP GOING ON!

GOODY!

THE GAULISH LADY TAKES GREAT CARE WITH HER MAKE-UP ...

I'M THE CHIEF AROUND HERE AND I CAN CALL ANYONE I LIKE A GREAT GOOF!

SPLOTCH!

I DUCKED! I DUCKED! YAH BOO SUCKS TO YOU!

L THIS MAKES THE AULISH LADY A DAINTY, ORABLE CREATURE ...

... SYMBOLIZING THE REFINEMENT OF THOSE WHOM HISTORIANS HAVE UNTHINKINGLY DESCRIBED AS BARBARIANS.

THE END

- UDERZO -
&
GOSCINNY.

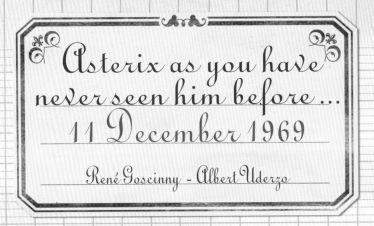

Asterix as you have never seen him before…
11 December 1969
René Goscinny - Albert Uderzo

These three pages of anthology pieces, which have kept all their force and originality, are very much in the spirit of "Pilote" magazine in the 1960s. The texts make their points tellingly and are very funny, while the drawing — or rather drawings — show a breathtaking mastery of many different graphic styles. How can an artist change his own style to caricature other strip cartoon illustrators so cleverly? There is a touch of the famous American "Mad" magazine here. The author has fun showing us what his imagination has come up with — for by agreement with René Goscinny, Albert both wrote and drew these three amazing pages by himself. A treat to be (re)discovered.

SINCE THE BIRTH OF ASTERIX, MANY OF OUR READERS AND CERTAIN SPECIALIST STRIP CARTOON MAGAZINES, NOT TO MENTION THE CRITICS, HAVE SUGGESTED IDEAS TO US. WE WOULD LIKE TO THANK THEM FOR THEIR KIND CONTRIBUTIONS, AND WE THOUGHT IT WOULD BE INTERESTING TO ADAPT ASTERIX IN LINE WITH SOME OF THEIR SUGGESTIONS.

SUGGESTION 1

"WHY DON'T YOU, LIKE, YOU KNOW, HAVE THE DRUID INVENTING MODERN GADGETS? THE CHARACTERS DON'T TALK, LIKE, NATURAL. AND EVEN WORSE, THE DRAWINGS JUST FOR KIDS, LIKE MICKEY MOUSE STUFF. SIGNED, A PAL."

SUGGESTION 2

"'STORIES TOO LONG' - STOP - 'TOO MUCH DIALOGUE' - STOP - 'NOT ENOUGH SIMPLICITY IN DRAWING' - STOP - 'WHY NOT TAKE ASTERIX TO AMERICA?' - STOP - SIGNED, PROFESSOR HEDDY, UNIVERSITY OF NANTES."

SUGGESTION 3

"THE LATEST ASTERIX BOOK WAS NOT TOO BAD, UNATTRACTIVE AND MUDDLED AS THE DRAWING WAS. ON THE OTHER HAND WE WERE DELIGHTED TO RE-READ THE WONDERFUL COLLECTION OF THE ADVENTURES OF THE HIGH-FLYING CRASH CORDON IN THE AMAZING WORLD OF DEEP SPACE."

FROM A REVIEW IN "PHOEBUS", THE JOURNAL OF ASCII (ASSOCIATION FOR STRIP CARTOON INFORMATION INTERCHANGE)

THANKS TO THE DRUID'S MAGIC AMPHORA, OUR HEROES ARRIVE ON MARS BY WAY OF JUPITER, JUNO AND MERCURY.

AND, BY TOUTATIS! MARS IS OUR LAST CHANCE TO FIND THE VERY ESSENCE OF LIFE, OBELYX!

EVER SINCE THEY DISAPPEARED FROM EART THE EXISTENCE OF OUR TRIBE HAS BEEN AT RISK!

AND WITH THEIR FIRST STEPS ON MARTIAN SOIL, THE MOMENT COMES...

ASTERYX! LOOK! THERE! WE'RE SAVED!

AT LAST! LOTS AND LOTS OF ROMANS! LOTS OF LOVELY ROMANS!

SUGGESTION 4

"I AM A SYCOPHANT AIMING TO PROMOTE CINEDOLOGICALLY NECROMANTIC SYMBIOSIS. MY EGO REBELS AGAINST YOUR WORK AND URGES DEHORTATION. THE CRETINOIDAL MICROCEPHALY OF YOUR PHYLACTERIO-LOGICAL TEXT, TOGETHER WITH THE MONSTROUS SPACIOSITY OF EMPIRICIST GRAPHICS SUGGESTING RETROSPECTIVE DELIRIUM, IS AN INSULT TO THE INTELLECT AND TO THE STUDY OF UNIVERSALS AS ENVISAGED AND CARRIED OUT BY THE MIND." HUBERT BLETHER, EDITOR, "THE LITERARY SYCOPHANT". (AUTHORS' NOTE: THIS SUGGESTION IS OBVIOUSLY FOR A WEIGHTIER AND MORE INTELLECTUAL TEXT.)

YOU SAY A GREAT MANY THINGS IN ATTEMPTING TO SEEM TO CONTRADICT ME, YET NONETHELESS YOU SAY NOTHING THAT CONTRADICTS ME SINCE YOU COME TO THE SAME CONCLUSION AS I DO. NONETHELESS YOU INTERPOSE IN CERTAIN PASSAGES SEVERAL REMARKS TO WHICH I CANNOT AGREE, FOR INSTANCE THAT THE AXIOM *THERE IS NOTHING IN AN EFFECT WHICH WAS NOT PREVIOUSLY IN ITS CAUSE* SHOULD BE UNDERSTOOD AS DENOTING THE MATERIAL CAUSE RATHER THAN THE EFFICACY, FOR IT IS IMPOSSIBLE TO CONCEIVE OF PERFECTION OF FORM PRE-EXISTING IN THE MATERIAL CAUSE, ONLY IN THE SOLE EFFICACIOUS CAUSE, AND ALSO YOU SAY THAT ...

... THE FORMAL REALITY OF AN IDEA IS A SUBSTANCE, WITH SEVERAL OTHER SIMILAR REMARKS. IF YOU HAD ANY EVIDENCE OF THE EXISTENCE OF MATERIAL THINGS THEN NO DOUBT YOU WOULD HAVE SET IT DOWN HERE. BUT SINCE YOU ASK ONLY, "IF IT IS THEREFORE TRUE THAT I AM NOT CERTAIN OF THE EXISTENCE OF ANYTHING BESIDES MYSELF IN THE WORLD," AND SINCE YOU PRETEND THERE IS NO NEED TO LOOK FOR REASONS FOR SOMETHING SO OBVIOUS, AND THUS YOU ARE REPORTING ONLY YOUR OLD PREJUDICES, YOU MAKE IT ALL THE MORE CLEAR THAT YOU HAVE NO REASONS ...

... PROVING WHAT YOU SAY, ANY MORE THAN IF YOU HAD NEVER SAID ANYTHING AT ALL. AS FOR WHAT YOU SAY ABOUT IDEAS, IT NEEDS NO REPLY BECAUSE YOU CONFINE THE TERM OF IDEA SOLELY TO IMAGES DEPICTED IN THE IMAGINATION, WHILE I UNDERSTAND IT AS ALL THAT WE CONCEIVE OF IN OUR THOUGHTS. HOWEVER, I WILL ASK, IN PASSING, WHAT ARGUMENT YOU CITE TO PROVE THAT "NOTHING ACTS UPON ITSELF", FOR IT IS NOT YOUR HABIT TO USE ARGUMENTS IN EVIDENCE OF WHAT YOU SAY. YOU MAY SAY YOU PROVE IT BY THE EXAMPLE OF THE FINGER WHICH CANNOT STRIKE ITSELF, AND THE EYE WHICH CANNOT SEE ITSELF EXCEPT IN A MIRROR, TO WHICH IT IS EASY TO REPLY THAT IT IS BY NO MEANS THE EYE WHICH SEES ITSELF OR THE MIRROR, BUT THE MIND, WHICH ALONE KNOWS BOTH THE MIRROR AND THE EYE AND ITSELF. ONE MAY EVEN CITE FURTHER EXAMPLES DRAWN FROM CORPOREAL MATTERS CONCERNING THE ACTION A THING MAY HAVE UPON ITSELF, AS WHEN A CURVED PLANE TURNS IN UPON ITSELF, FOR IS NOT THAT CONVERSION AN ACTION EXERCISED UPON ITSELF?*

* REPLIES TO OBJECTION V TO THE MEDITATIONS OF DESCARTES.

?!?!?!?!?! !?!?!?!?!? ?!?!?!?!?! !?!?!?!?!?

THANKS TO THE DRUID'S MAGIC FLOWERS, WE CAN NOW DO A PROPER JOB OF FIGHTING THE WILD WOMEN WARRIORS LED BY PROCONSULESS DEODORA, OBELIX!

WE HAVE ONLY TO BRUSH THEM GENTLY WITH THESE FLOWERS, SO GETAFIX TOLD ME. WATCH OUT! THEY'RE ATTACKING!

IF YOU ASK ME, ASTERIX, THIS ISN'T AS MUCH FUN AS A GOOD PUNCH-UP!

HERE IS THE LAST SUGGESTION, THE ONE WHICH WE, THE AUTHORS, WOULD LIKE TO PUT TO YOU, OUR READERS. IT'S A QUESTION OF AESTHETICS, WHICH JUST SUDDENLY CAME TO US. A DARING IDEA, WE ADMIT, BUT ALL THE SAME WE KNOW OUR CHARACTERS WELL, I MEAN WE MADE THEM UP, DIDN'T WE? SO WE HAVE A RIGHT TO HAVE IDEAS TOO, OH YES WE DO! OH, REALLY, WE DON'T BELIEVE IT!?! SHUT UP! WE'RE FREE AGENTS, AREN'T WE? VERY WELL, IF THAT'S HOW YOU LOT FEEL, IN FUTURE ASTERIX AND OBELIX WILL WEAR PLUS-FOURS...

HONESTLY! I MEAN, I ASK YOU! THESE AUTHORS ARE CRAZY!

TAP! TAP! TAP!

TAP! TAP! TAP!

— UDERZO.

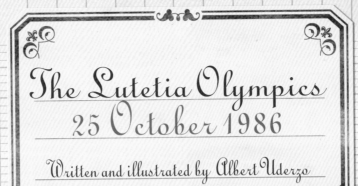

The Lutetia Olympics
25 October 1986

Written and illustrated by Albert Uderzo

In the mid-1980s the mayor of Paris turned to Asterix for help in its Olympic bid. Jacques Chirac and his municipal team wanted Paris (the former city of Lutetia) to stage the AD 1992 Games.

Albert Uderzo was asked to create a poster and a small four-page strip cartoon story to win support from the Parisii tribe of Lutetia. He liked the idea, and designed a poster which went up all over the capital in 1986. The story was published in "Jours de France", a popular magazine of the last century. In the end the Olympic Committee did not award the Games to Paris, but obviously not everyone lost out, since just for the record, the original of the poster was never returned to the artist! But never mind: here you can see the Eiffel Tower turned into a huge, magnificent dovecote and a really nasty villain is added to the rogues' gallery of the Asterix stories.

"Jours de France", n° 1660

PEACE TEMPORARILY REIGNS BETWEEN THE GAULS OF ASTERIX'S LITTLE VILLAGE AND THE ROMANS GARRISONING THE NEARBY FORTIFIED CAMPS.

A MESSAGE BY EXPRESS CARRIER! LET US BEND ...

... OUR MINDS TO ITS CONTENTS!

CLANG!

IT WAS ONLY A FIGURE OF SPEECH, YOU FOOLS!!!

PFFFF!

GWRLF!

RIGHT, YOU TWO JOKERS! LISTEN TO THIS MESSAGE SIGNED BY PARTIPOLITIX, CHIEF OF THE PARISII TRIBE* IN LUTETIA!

PFFF!

* GAULS LIVING IN LUTETIA WHO LATER GAVE THEIR NAME TO PARIS.

"EXACTLY 100 YEARS AGO A GAULISH ATHLETE CALLED PIERRE DECOUBERTIX WON AT THE OLYMPIC GAMES IN GREECE. IT WAS THE FIRST TIME A NON-GREEK ATHLETE HAD EVER BEEN CROWNED WITH THE LAUREL WREATH OF VICTORY. TO COMMEMORATE THIS EVENT, THE OLYMPIC COMMITTEE HAS DECIDED TO HOLD ITS NEXT GAMES OUTSIDE GREECE!"

PFFFFF!

"SEVERAL GREAT CITIES OF THE ANCIENT WORLD HAVE PUT IN BIDS TO HOST THE GAMES. IT WOULD BE ONLY RIGHT FOR THEM TO BE HELD IN LUTETIA, THE GAULISH CAPITAL. WE MUST THEREFORE PERSUADE THE DELEGATES OF THE OLYMPIC COMMITTEE WHO ARE COMING TO VISIT US TO AWARD THE CITY THAT HONOUR!"

PFFFF!

BONG BONG!

"ROME HAS ALSO MADE A BID FOR THE GAMES. JULIUS CAESAR IS SURE TO CAUSE TROUBLE TO ENSURE THAT ROME GETS CHOSEN. SO I AM ASKING THE VILLAGE OF INDOMITABLE GAULS TO HELP US. PLEASE SEND YOUR MOST COURAGEOUS WARRIORS! THE HONOUR OF GAUL IS AT STAKE!"

PFFFFF!

WE ARE YOUR MOST COURAGEOUS WARRIORS, O CHIEF VITALSTATISTIX!

TRUE, ASTERIX, BUT TELL YOUR COURAGEOUS FRIEND TO STOP LAUGHING IN THAT SILLY WAY! THE HONOUR OF THE VILLAGE IS AT STAKE!

PFFFAH!AH!AH!

FOR ONLY ROME MUST BE RECOGNIZED AS THE OLYMPIC CAPITAL!

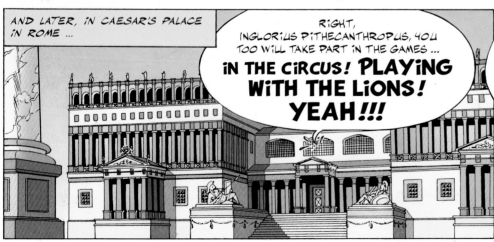

Springtime in Gaul
17 March 1966

René Goscinny – Albert Uderzo

René Goscinny, overworked at the time, asked Albert if he had any ideas for a story about spring. For the second time Albert wrote a little story of his own and showed it to his colleague before he drew the pictures.

René was delighted with the magical seasons, so Albert created this two-page story on his own, as well as the cover picture of the magazine. Albert was inspired by his childhood, when he loved walking from the Faubourg Saint-Antoine to Aligre market near the Bastille in Paris, where the costermongers sold fruit and vegetables from their barrows. René simply suggested to his friend the part played by Obelix in the final delightful gag.

"Pilote", n° 334

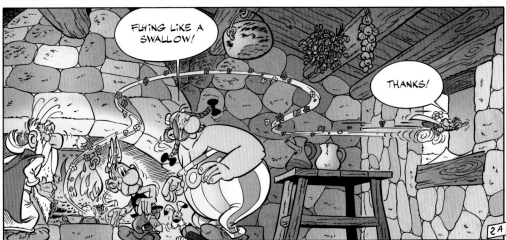

The mascot
13 June 1968

Written by   Illustrated by
René Goscinny   -   Albert Uderzo

The story of "The mascot" was originally published in the smaller format of the "Super Pocket Pilote" series, and in a magazine commissioned by the town council of Romainville — one of the suburbs of Lutetia. With a name like that — "Roman-town" — it was not surprising that the council should invite Asterix and his friends to pay a visit. In this complete story, full of the familiar features of the Asterix adventures, Dogmatix is kidnapped. Obelix's little friend, who first appeared in "Asterix and the Banquet", soon became one of the favourite characters in the village. Here he is the victim of his own charms — after all, anyone would want a little dog who was so keen on preserving the environment twenty centuries ahead of his time!

It was all thanks to Dogmatix that Obelix stopped uprooting trees and became ecologixally conscious!

"SuperPocket Pilote", n°1

the mascot

TEXT BY
GOSCINNY

DRAWN BY
UDERZO

ABSOLUTELY, ASTERIX! I TELL YOU DOGMATIX IS A GREAT LITTLE DOG! THE TROUBLE IS YOU DON'T TRUST HIM. IT GIVES HIM AN INFERIORITY COMPLEX!*

NEVER MIND THAT. LOOK WHO'S HERE!

* THE ORIGIN OF THE MODERN COMPLEX.

...O SHOULD BE HERE BUT A FINE STANDING ROMAN PATROL?

WHO ...ULS!

NOT **THE** TWO GAULS?!

DULCE ET DECORUM EST PRO PATRIA MORI.

SHUT UP, IGNORAMUS!

ON SUCH A FINE DAY IN THE ARMORICAN FOREST, WE WILL NOT DWELL ON THE FEW SECONDS OF VIOLENCE PRECEDING THE SCENE NOW SHOWN BELOW.

HONESTLY, THEY'RE GOING TOO FAR!

WE DIDN'T DO A THING TO THOSE CHAUVINIST GAULISH BOORS! ALL WE DID WAS INVADE THEM!

VICTRIX CAUSA DIIS PLACUIT, SED VICTA CATONI!

IF YOU'RE QUITE THROUGH WITH THE CLASSICAL QUOTATIONS ...

NUNC EST BIBENDUM.

ALL THAT FOREST TO PATROL AND WE HAVE TO RUN INTO THOSE SOCIAL MISFITS! WE'RE DOWN ON OUR LUCK!

OH, LEAVE IT OUT!

YOU KNOW WHY WE'RE DOWN ON OUR LUCK?

WHY?

...R, QUID, ...OMODO?

YOU'RE BEGINNING TO GET ME DOWN, YOU ARE!

BECAUSE WE DON'T HAVE A MASCOT!

A MASCOT?

OF COURSE! WE NEED A MASCOT! OUR MATES BACK HOME ON THE CAPITOL HAVE THE SACRED GEESE. THOSE GEESE TURNED OUT GOOD EGGS!

RES, NON VERBA.

YOU ASKED FOR IT!

HE'S GOT A RIGHT TO SPEAK LATIN GRAMMAR!

JUST WATCH HIM PARSING THROUGH!

PAF!

I'M GOING TO LOOK FOR A LITTLE ANIMAL TO BE OUR MASCOT!

I'M SURE TO FIND A LITTLE ...IMAL SOMEWHERE ...N THIS FOREST.

AT THAT VERY MOMENT...

WATCH THIS! THEN YOU'LL SEE WHAT A GREAT LITTLE DOG MY DOGMATIX IS!

WHAT DO YOU EXPECT YOUR GREAT LITTLE DOGMATIX TO DO?

FETCH, DOGMATIX!

44

45

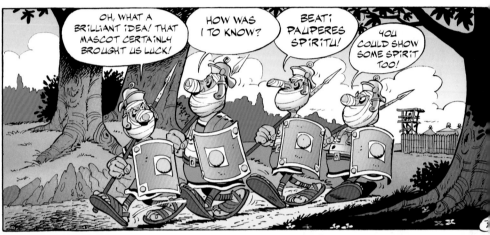

Latinomania
March 1973

Written by · Illustrated by
René Goscinny — Albert Uderzo

Thirty years ago, amused by the campaign against the use of English words in French — a phenomenon known as "franglais" — René Goscinny decided to use the Gauls to poke fun at it. He replied indirectly and humorously to the famous author Maurice Druon, one of the keenest to defend the purity of French, by imagining a similar fashion for "Latinisms" in occupied Gaul, and wrote this story, drawn by Albert Uderzo. It will certainly teach you more Latin than the other stories in this collection, by Toutatis!

This story, entitled "Latinomania" or "Et cetera", has been completely re-inked and re-coloured, like most of the stories here that date from the 1960s. Below is the cover of the first edition of the book you are now reading, published in France in 1993. Four hundred thousand copies were sold within weeks. However, it has never before been published in English, so all fourteen stories are new to readers of Asterix on the other side of the Channel.

Just for the record, on 10 August 1993, the day the first edition (in a giftbox with the videos of the first Asterix films) was released, the French publishers' switchboards crashed. The success of the book, which sold far more copies than the most optimistic had expected, persuaded us to promise a new, improved and longer edition to the readers and booksellers who have been waiting eagerly for it. Would we ever give in to blackmail? By Toutatis, no! But here at last is the book!

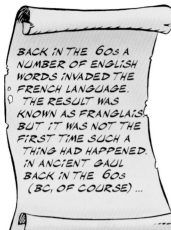

BACK IN THE 60s A NUMBER OF ENGLISH WORDS INVADED THE FRENCH LANGUAGE. THE RESULT WAS KNOWN AS FRANGLAIS, BUT IT WAS NOT THE FIRST TIME SUCH A THING HAD HAPPENED. IN ANCIENT GAUL BACK IN THE 60s (BC, OF COURSE) ...

HEY, YOU TWO! KEEP OFF MY GERANIUMS!

OOPS! MEA CULPA!

YOU MIGHT PAY A MINIMUM OF ATTENTION!

A LITTLE DECORUM, PLEASE, DEAR!

THERE'S NO NEED TO SHOUT! THIS ISN'T A FORUM OR AN AUDITORIUM!

ME, SHOUTING? IT'S YOU SHOUTING! SHUT UP, AND THAT'S AN ULTIMATUM!

ULTIMATUM? WE'LL SEE ABOUT THAT!

NO! NOT THE AQUARIUM!

I HEARD ALL THAT! IT'S A CRYING SHAME. SPEAKING LATIN! WE MUST PRESERVE THE PURITY OF OUR BEAUTIFUL GAULISH LANGUAGE!

SPEAKING LATIN? US?

GLUG GLUGGLUG GLUG GLUG?

THAT'S RIGHT. AUDITORIUM, ULTIMATUM, AQUARIUM: THEY'RE ALL LATIN WORDS!

BUT WHAT OUGHT WE TO SAY INSTEAD, O DRUID?

WELL, "HALL FOR PUBLIC PERFORMANCES", "FINAL DEMAND ALLOWING NO ARGUMENT", "GLASS CONTAINER FOR FRESH-WATER OR SALT-WATER FISH" ...

ETCETERA, ETCETERA.

UDERZO & GOSCINNY

48

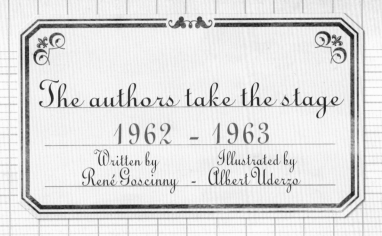

The authors take the stage
1962 - 1963

Written by
René Goscinny

Illustrated by
Albert Uderzo

Although strip cartoons tend to be written and drawn to a standard pattern today, in the 1960s and 1970s there was more of a libertarian spirit in them, and they often ignored graphic conventions and logical time schemes. Showing the authors in the company of their own creations was almost obligatory — readers expected and wanted it, and indeed that was one of the reasons for the magical sympathy between readers and authors.

It was in this spirit that René and Albert, like many other writers and illustrators of strip cartoons, invented works of pure fantasy in which they crossed the borders of space and time, and finally revealed the true story of the creation of Asterix.

* The power to make people laugh: from an epigram by Caesar on Terence, the Latin poet.

The Obelix family tree
07 February 1963

Written by
René Goscinny

Illustrated by
Albert Uderzo

(This story was first
published in 15 issues
of "Pilote", n.os 172–186

A FEW DAYS AGO TWO FRIENDS WHO ARE ALSO COLLEAGUES WERE TAKING A QUIET WALK ALONG THE SEA FRONT IN A LITTLE HARBOUR TOWN IN BRITTANY ...

...WHEN...

LOOK AT THAT!

HMMH?

INCREDIBLE!

IMPOSSIBLE!

AN AMAZING LIKENESS! WHAT A COINCIDENCE!

COINCIDENCE? MAYBE NOT ... LET'S FOLLOW HIM!

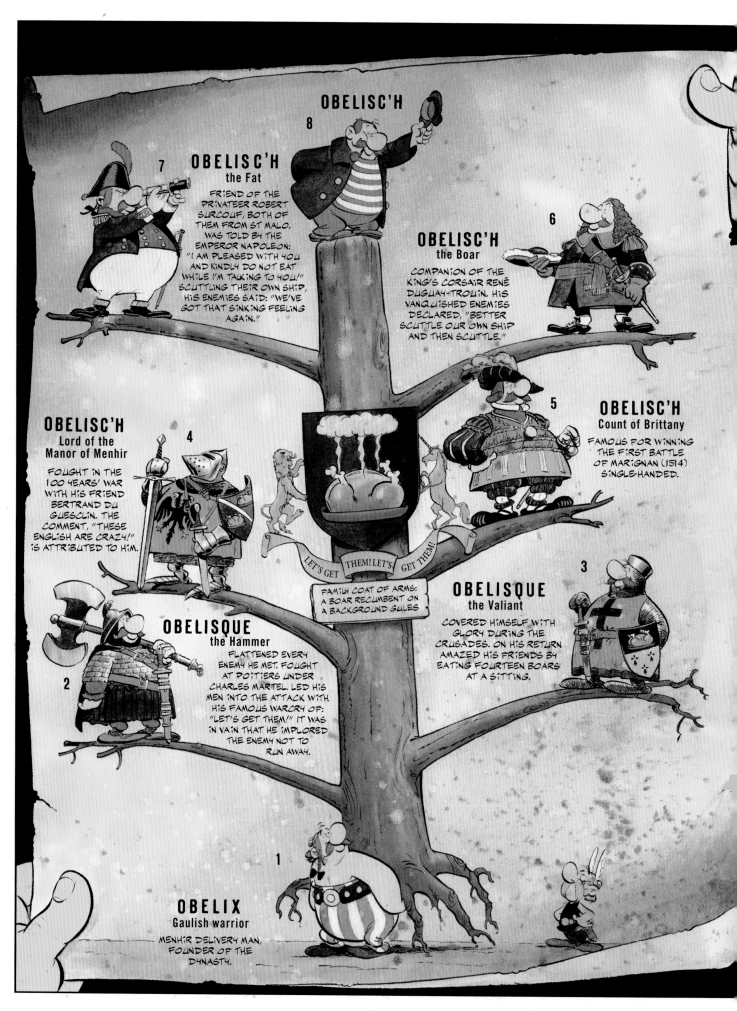

OBELISC'H

8

OBELISC'H
the Fat

FRIEND OF THE PRIVATEER ROBERT SURCOUF, BOTH OF THEM FROM ST MALO. WAS TOLD BY THE EMPEROR NAPOLEON: "I AM PLEASED WITH YOU AND KINDLY DO NOT EAT WHILE I'M TALKING TO YOU!" SCUTTLING THEIR OWN SHIP, HIS ENEMIES SAID: "WE'VE GOT THAT SINKING FEELING AGAIN."

7

OBELISC'H
the Boar

COMPANION OF THE KING'S CORSAIR RENÉ DUGUAY-TROUIN. HIS VANQUISHED ENEMIES DECLARED, "BETTER SCUTTLE OUR OWN SHIP AND THEN SCUTTLE."

6

OBELISC'H
Lord of the
Manor of Menhir

FOUGHT IN THE 100 YEARS' WAR WITH HIS FRIEND BERTRAND DU GUESCLIN. THE COMMENT, "THESE ENGLISH ARE CRAZY!" IS ATTRIBUTED TO HIM.

4

OBELISC'H
Count of Brittany

FAMOUS FOR WINNING THE FIRST BATTLE OF MARIGNAN (1514) SINGLE-HANDED.

5

LET'S GET THEM! LET'S GET THEM!

FAMILY COAT OF ARMS: A BOAR RECUMBENT ON A BACKGROUND GULES

OBELISQUE
the Hammer

FLATTENED EVERY ENEMY HE MET. FOUGHT AT POITIERS UNDER CHARLES MARTEL. LED HIS MEN INTO THE ATTACK WITH HIS FAMOUS WARCRY OF: "LET'S GET THEM!" IT WAS IN VAIN THAT HE IMPLORED THE ENEMY NOT TO RUN AWAY.

2

OBELISQUE
the Valiant

COVERED HIMSELF WITH GLORY DURING THE CRUSADES. ON HIS RETURN AMAZED HIS FRIENDS BY EATING FOURTEEN BOARS AT A SITTING.

3

OBELIX
Gaulish warrior

MENHIR DELIVERY MAN, FOUNDER OF THE DYNASTY.

1

THE END

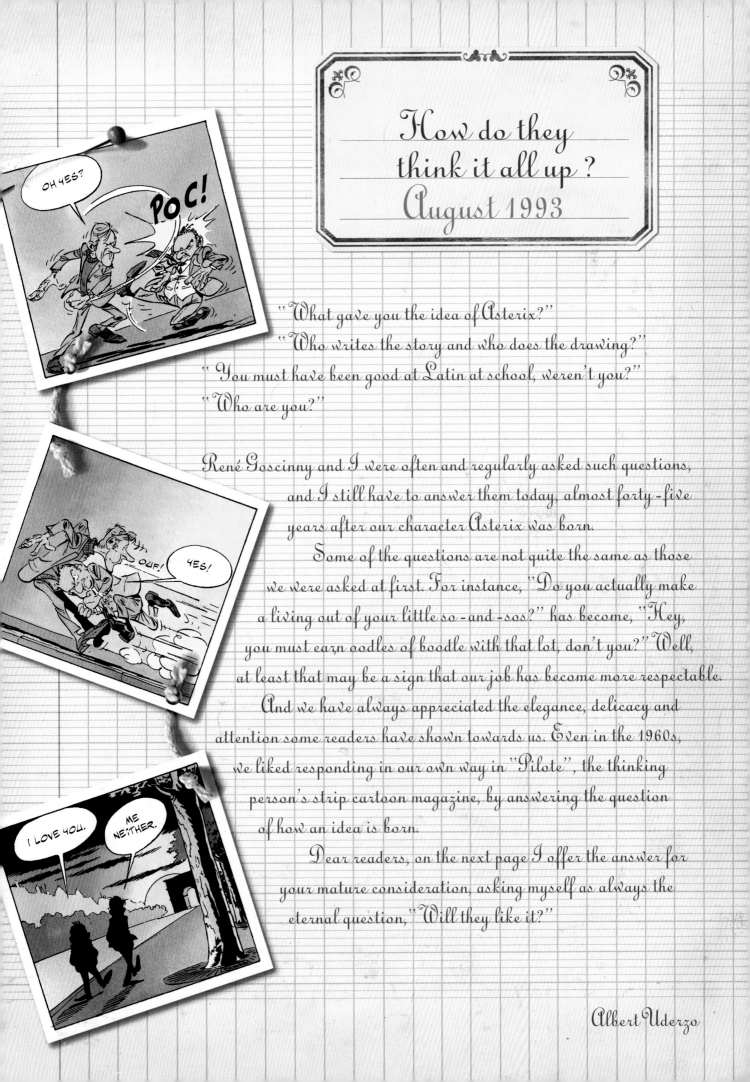

"What gave you the idea of Asterix?"
"Who writes the story and who does the drawing?"
"You must have been good at Latin at school, weren't you?"
"Who are you?"

René Goscinny and I were often and regularly asked such questions, and I still have to answer them today, almost forty-five years after our character Asterix was born.

Some of the questions are not quite the same as those we were asked at first. For instance, "Do you actually make a living out of your little so-and-sos?" has become, "Hey, you must earn oodles of boodle with that lot, don't you?" Well, at least that may be a sign that our job has become more respectable. And we have always appreciated the elegance, delicacy and attention some readers have shown towards us. Even in the 1960s, we liked responding in our own way in "Pilote", the thinking person's strip cartoon magazine, by answering the question of how an idea is born.

Dear readers, on the next page I offer the answer for your mature consideration, asking myself as always the eternal question, "Will they like it?"

Albert Uderzo

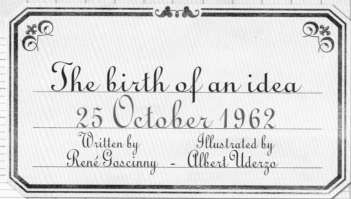

The birth of an idea
25 October 1962

Written by
René Goscinny

Illustrated by
Albert Uderzo

"Pilote", n° 157

JON AGEE

THE
WALL
IN THE
MIDDLE
OF THE
BOOK

Scallywag Press Ltd
LONDON

There's a wall in the middle of the book.

'A book that celebrates
freedom of movement and thought.'

AMNESTY INTERNATIONAL

First published in Great Britain in 2019 by Scallywag Press Ltd,
10 Sutherland Row, London SW1V 4JT

Published by arrangement with Dial Books for Young Readers, an
imprint of Penguin Young Readers Group, a division of Penguin
Random House LLC

Printed on FSC paper in Malaysia by Tien Wah Press

001

British Library Cataloguing in Publication Data available

978-1-912650-04-0

And it's a good thing.

The wall protects this side of the book . . .

from the other side of the book.

This side of the book is safe.

The other side is not.

But the most dangerous thing
on the other side of the book
is the ogre.

If the ogre ever caught me, he'd eat me up.

That's why I'm glad there's a wall
in the middle of the book,
and that I'm on this side of it.

Wait a second. What's going on?!

This is not supposed to happen
on this side of the wall!

Wow!
Thank you so much!

OH NO!
I'm on the other side of the book!

And you're the ogre who's going to eat me up!

Haw-haw-haw! I'm actually a nice ogre.
And this side of the book is fantastic!

Come on, I'll show you around!

Hey, ogre! Wait for me!